First published in 2000 by
Cat's Whiskers
96 Leonard Street
London EC2A 4XD

Cat's Whiskers Australia
14 Mars Road
Lane Cove
NSW 2066

ISBN 1 90301 214 7 (hbk)
ISBN 1 90301 215 5 (pbk)

Originally published by K. Thienemanns Verlag, Stuttgart, Vienna, Berne
Copyright © K. Thienemanns Verlag 1999
English text copyright © Cat's Whiskers 2000

A CIP catalogue record for this book is available from the British Library

Printed in Belgium

ED LOVES SARAH LOVES TIM

by Edith Schreiber-Wicke   illustrated by Carola Holland

CAT'S Whiskers
THE WATTS PUBLISHING GROUP LTD

At first, Ed wasn't sure what it was.

He felt a bit sick in his tummy, and there was a strange whooshing sound in his ears.

Then he realised...

it happened every time Sarah looked at him!

Suddenly, Ed couldn't wait
to get up in the morning.

He jumped out of bed,
and ate his breakfast
without complaining once.

"You never used to like going to school
this much," said his Mum.

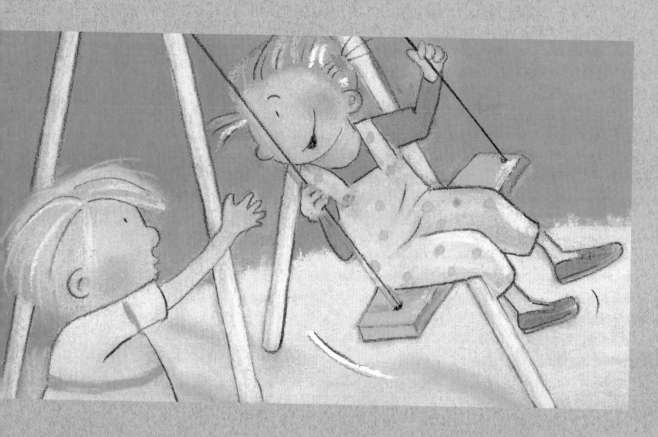

A few days later, in the playground,
Sarah asked Ed,
"Will you be be my boy-friend?"

She took Ed by the hand.
It was a wonderful feeling!

As Ed walked home with his Mum,
the whole world seemed to be smiling at him.

The air was a lovely warm colour,
and Ed imagined he could see
happy teddies everywhere.

Sarah liked to talk a lot, and when she was angry she shouted. But the best thing she ever said was, "Ed is my boy-friend!"

And she said that often.

It was great!
Ed's Mum liked
Sarah's Mum,
and Ed's Dad liked
Sarah's Dad...

which meant that Ed could see Sarah
at the weekends, too.

And even when it rained it was wonderful,
because they could stay indoors and play
cards together.

But suddenly everything
went horribly wrong.

The day began badly.

Ed's breakfast mug
fell on the floor.

Then he lost his shoe.

Worst of all,
Ed tripped coming down
the stairs and hurt his knee.

That day Ed
was late for school.

When Ed arrived,
Sarah was already sitting
in a circle with the others.
She had Tim on one side
and Hannah on the other.

Ed had to sit a long
way away from her.

Sarah was busy talking to Tim, and didn't
even seem to notice that Ed had arrived.

Later, when they went into the garden,
Sarah held Tim's hand.

"Where's Sarah?" asked Ed's Mum
when she came to collect him.

Ed didn't answer. He put on his
shoes and headed for the door.

"Don't you want to wait for Sarah?"
his Mum asked.
Ed shook his head.
"She loves Tim now."

Ed's Mum didn't say any more.
She just gave Ed an extra little hug.

Ed hated Tim.
He wanted him to turn into a bat,
or a toad, or a big ugly pig.

Sarah was frightened of pigs.

But Ed didn't know any magic spells,
so Tim was still Tim the next day,
and all the sad days that followed.

Ed stood and looked out of the window.

Outside in the street, people were
walking their dogs.

They came in all shapes and all sizes,
but they were always special friends.

Everyone seemed to have
a special friend, except him.

But one day, just as suddenly,
everything changed again.

Ed was late for school, and when
he got there Hannah was already
at the board spelling a word.
Ed noticed that her ginger hair
was really bright and shiny.

Then Hannah turned to face
Ed, and smiled at him.
Ed couldn't believe it -
there was that same
feeling again!

A bit sick in his tummy,
and a strange whooshing
sound in his ears...